All Tied Up

Tony Bradman ● Jon Stuart

Contents

OXFO
UNIVERSITY

Macro Marvel
(billionaire inventor)

Welcome to Micro World!

Macro Marvel invented Micro World – a micro-sized theme park where you have to shrink to get in.

A computer called **CODE** controls Micro World and all the robots inside – MITEs and BITEs.

A MITE

A BITE

Disaster strikes!

CODE goes wrong on opening day.
CODE wants to shrink the world.

Macro Marvel is trapped inside the park ...

Enter Team X!

Four micro agents – **Max, Cat, Ant** and **Tiger** – are sent to rescue Macro Marvel and defeat CODE.

Mini Marvel joins Team X.

Mini Marvel
(Macro's daughter)

In the last book ...

- Cat made a whirlpool to make the Octo-BITE dizzy.
- Cat and Tiger tried to unscrew the CODE key from the Octo-BITE.
- The Octo-BITE blasted Tiger with poison ink!

**CODE key
(5 collected)**

You are in the Shark Dive zone.

3

Before you read

Sound checker
Say the sounds.

aw   **au**

Sound spotter
Blend the sounds.

j	aw

s	or	t	s

h	au	l	ed

l	au	n	ch

Tricky words
different
laughed

Into the zone

The BITE shot ink at Tiger. What do you think might happen next?

4

A Cure for Tiger

Cat hauled Tiger into the Shark Sub.
"I saw the Octo-BITE shoot poison
ink at him!" she gasped, her jaw
wide open.

Tiger's arm hurt.
"I'll look for a cure on my
Gizmo," said Mini.

Cure for poison ink

Shark Dive

Rub the skin with different sorts of seaweed.

"I saw some seaweed on the sea bed," said Ant.
Mini sent a MITE to find the seaweed.

The MITE hauled the seaweed
into the Shark Sub.
Mini rubbed Tiger's arm.
"It tickles!" laughed Tiger.

Suddenly, the screen in the Shark Sub crackled. It was a text from CODE to the Octo-BITE.

Stop Team X! Launch an attack now!

Now you have read ...
A Cure for Tiger

Take a closer look

Look at page 9. Which word tells you how Tiger is speaking?
Can you change your voice when you read this so it sounds like Tiger?

Look on page 5 for another word that tells you how Cat is speaking.

It tickles!

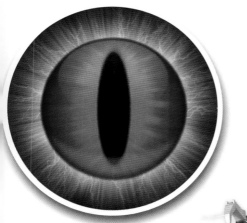

Thinking time

What do you know about CODE?
Why does CODE want to stop Team X?

I must stop Team X!

Before you read

Sound checker
Say the sounds.

aw   au

Sound spotter
Blend the sounds.

s	aw

m	au	l

or	d	er	ed

Tricky words
different
laughed

Into the zone
What do you think the
Octo-BITE might do next?

12

In the Net

Mini was feeling sad.
"We'll never find my dad," she said.
"Don't worry," said Max. "We'll beat this BITE and find your dad soon."

Suddenly, Cat saw the BITE. "The BITE is trying to get in the sub!" she cried.

The BITE tried to maul the sub with its tentacles.

"I will stop the BITE with my force shield," said Max.

He swam out of the Shark Sub.

Max hooked his wire around the Shark Sub's tooth. He was hauled along as the sub moved.

Max put up his force shield.

The Octo-BITE had to let go.
Now it chased the sub.

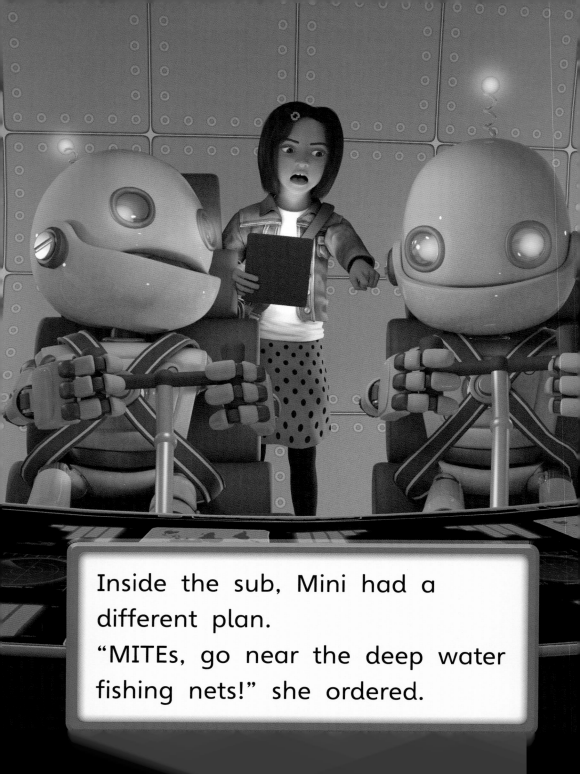

Inside the sub, Mini had a different plan.
"MITEs, go near the deep water fishing nets!" she ordered.

The BITE got tangled in the nets.

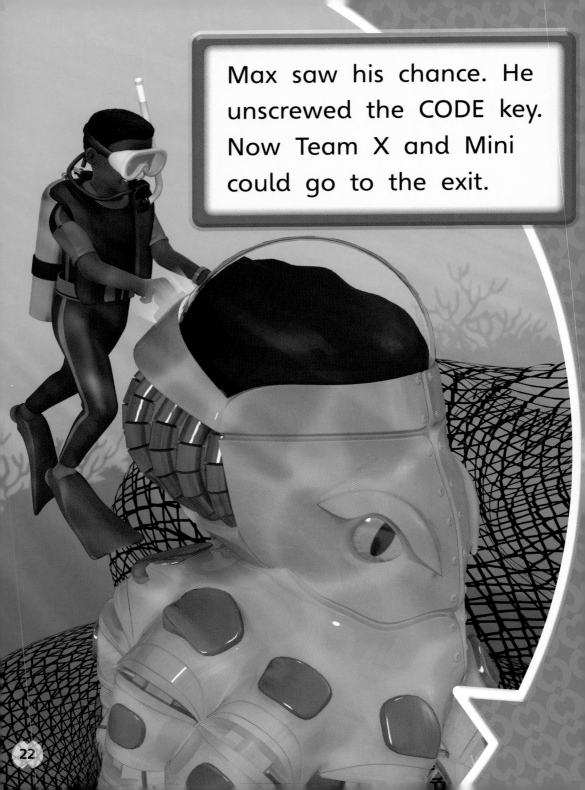

Max saw his chance. He unscrewed the CODE key. Now Team X and Mini could go to the exit.

Max put in the CODE key.
"Ha! We showed that BITE!
Now we have six CODE keys!"
laughed Tiger.

Now you have read ...
In the Net

To get to the next zone we have to read the CODE words. Then the exit door will open. Can you help us read them?

sead	quirse
virm	shroup
snew	fawl
bowse	gauzz